Love Potion

Magical Midlife Series
By
Rose Bak

Love Potion

Magical Midlife Romance, Volume 1

Rose Bak

Published by Rose Bak, 2022.

Table of Contents

LOVE POTION

© 2022 by Rose Bak

ALL RIGHTS RESERVED. No portion of this book may be reproduced, transmitted, downloaded, decompiled, reverse engineered, or stored in or introduced into any information storage retrieval system in any form by any means without express permission from the publisher, except as permitted by U.S. copyright law. For permissions contact the publisher at rosebakenterprises@msn.com.

Warning: the unauthorized reproduction or distribution of this copyrighted work is illegal. Criminal copyright infringement, including infringement without monetary gain, is investigated by the FBI and is punishable by up to 5 years in prison and a fine of $250,000.

This is a work of fiction. Names, characters, places, and incidents are either the product of the author's imagination or are used fictitiously. Any resemblance to actual persons, living or dead, events, organizations, or locals is entirely coincidental. Trademark names are used editorially with no infringement of the respective owner's trademark. All activities depicted occur between consenting characters 18 years or older who are not blood related.

Cover art by Paper or Pixels

About This Book

The love spell worked...on the wrong sister!

When her sister begs her to do a love spell to attract her true mate, Cami is hesitant. Her magic is glitchy on a good day. But what's the harm of trying? To everyone's shock, the spell manifests exactly the man they hoped for, except for one problem...he's in love with Cami, not her sister.

Shapeshifter Stephen doesn't believe in magic, but he does believe in fate. His wolf knows the truth: Cami is his true mate, the one he's destined to be together with forever. If only Cami could forget about the spell and listen to her heart...

"Love Potion" is a steamy standalone featuring a midlife couple, matchmaking sisters, and a little touch of magic leading to a happy ending.

This book includes a special excerpt from "Until You Came Along", book one of the Oliver Boys Rockstar series, available now from all major online retailers.

Join My Mailing List

Join Rose Bak's mailing list by visiting her website at www.AuthorRoseBak.com. You'll get a free book and be the first to hear about all the latest releases and special sales.

Dedication

For everyone who needs a little magic in their lives.

Prologue—Cami

"Come on, Cami! You're the only one who can help me."

"Pepper, you know what Mom always said. We shouldn't mess around with magic unless we really know what we're doing."

"You're a witch. You do know what you're doing."

I shook my head as I looked at my younger sister. I couldn't decide if she really had that much faith in my abilities, such as they were, or if she was just blowing smoke up my you-know-what to get me to give her what she wanted. Maybe a bit of both.

My two sisters and I were the product of a mixed marriage. Mom was a witch and Dad was human, but not a normal, he was also a psychic. The pairing had affected all of us differently. I had some magical tendences, although they tended to glitch a lot. Our youngest sister Meri was psychic. At least kind of psychic. Most of her visons were pretty useless to be honest. She could predict that you'd break your phone screen tomorrow, but she couldn't predict the lottery numbers or anything that was actually helpful. And Pepper, our middle sister, didn't seem to have any powers. At least none that we'd discovered so far.

"You know the first rule of witchcraft Pepper. Do no harm." Our mother had drilled that into us over and over when we were growing up.

"How would opening the path for my true love to find me do harm?" Pepper cocked her head to the side and gave me the entreating look she'd perfected way back when we were kids. "I'm thirty-four years old, I want to find my true love before my eggs shrivel up and I can't have kids anymore. The clock is ticking here."

I sighed. She'd been bugging me about this for weeks and I was tired of arguing with her.

"Fine, I'll do a spell." I held up a finger as my sister squealed with delight. "But I'll only do a spell to clear the path for you to find your true love, if the universe has one identified for you. But you need to be prepared that if there's no one destined to be with you, or the time isn't right for you to find your mate, the spell won't work."

"Fine, I get it, Chamomile. Whatever. Just hook me up and I'll take care of the rest."

I shot her a glare at her use of my full name. Our mom was...eccentric. As a witch, she used a lot of herbs and medicinal plants. For some reason that made her think it would be a good idea to name us all after plants. As if our lives weren't weird enough already.

"Kiss my ass, Peppermint."

Pepper rolled her eyes. "When can you do it?"

"The new moon is in a couple of days. I'll look up what we need and then we can do it by the river. We'll get Meri to help."

"Turmeric is a fuddy duddy. She never wants to do spells." Our youngest sister Meri was the least spiritual of all of us.

"She'll help, don't worry."

A few days later we three sisters gathered on the bank of the river that ran through the back of our family's land. The Rosewaters had lived on this land for over a hundred years, and each generation passed the land onto the next. Our mother and her sister had grown up here, and while Aunt Pat had moved away from the craziness of our magical world, Mom had raised us here. She and Dad were retired now and traveling the world, so we had the place to ourselves.

Some people thought it was weird for three grown women in their thirties to live together in their family home, but we weren't crazy. Rosewater Manor was huge, and we all had our own suites. Best of all, we owned it outright so there was no mortgage to pay. The house was well-equipped and came with household staff who did most of the cooking and cleaning, paid for by the large trust fund my mom had inherited from her parents. There was no way any of us would trade in a crappy one-bedroom apartment for the easy luxury of the Manor. Not unless we had a reason to, anyway.

The night was dark and clear as my sisters and I walked through the woods on our property and headed for the river. We found a flat space on the ground to set up. Using our flashlights to help us see, we quickly created a circle made from river stones, and the three of us settled inside the circle. Pepper and Meri built a small fire in the center of the circle while I gathered the other supplies for the spell, stopping a couple of times to refer to the notes on my phone. I didn't want to mess things up and summon my sister a demon instead of a husband.

"OK, we're ready."

We held hands and closed our eyes, slowing our breaths just as our mother had taught us. I began to draw forth the powers of my magic.

"Pepper, tell the universe what you'd like in a mate."

"He should be tall, dark, and handsome. Broad like a football player."

"Bring a mate who is tall," I intoned. "Bring a mate with hair like a raven. Bring a mate who is strong of body and handsome to the eye."

"Oh, and I want someone who's an animal in the sheets."

I rolled my eyes, not that Pepper could see it when we all had our eyes closed, and dutifully added, "Bring a mate who has animal tendencies."

I threw the magical herbs into the fire as I chanted the spell incantation. Turning my inner gaze up to my third eye – the space between my eyebrows—I tried to visualize the man my sister wanted to find. In my mind's eye I conjured a tall, broad man with wide shoulders and strong legs. I imagined dark hair and dark eyes, a man who was both wild and kind. I pressed my hands into the Earth and felt the light hum of magic thrumming though my fingertips.

"So shall it be."

Cami

A few days had passed since we'd done the spell in the woods. Pepper had been insufferable since then. During the day she roamed around town, hoping to run into her future husband, and at night she badgered me non-stop about if I thought the spell would work and how long it would take for someone to find her. It was as if she thought there was some kind of "thirty days or your money back" guarantee on magic.

On the third day I invited Pepper and Meri to go for a hike to take everyone's mind off the spell. Summer was coming and it was a warm, sunny day. Our family property backed up onto the woods, making it a perfect access point to a variety of trails through the forest. It was a warm, sunny day and the woods were alive with the smells and sounds of Spring. We'd been hiking for about half an hour when Meri suddenly stopped and clutched her head, a sure sign she was having one of her psychic visions.

"The wolf. It slips its collar."

Pepper and I looked at each other, then back at our sister. That was weird, even for Meri.

"What did you see?" Pepper asked her curiously.

Meri shook her head, then froze, her eyes wide. Shakily she raised one hand and pointed behind us. "That."

I turned around to look in the direction Meri was pointed, and gasped as I saw a wolf stalking towards us. It was the largest wolf I'd ever seen, but its eyes looked human. Oh thank the Goddess, it was just a wolf shifter not a real wild wolf. We knew shifters wouldn't hurt us. Our little town seemed to attract all manner of magical creatures, including shape shifters.

"What's up, Wolfie?" I asked as the wolf stopped in front of me, staring up at me intently.

The air around us shimmered. Cracking and popping noises filled the air and in an instant, the wolf in front of me changed into a man. A naked man. A hot as hell naked man.

"Mate!" he growled, his deep voice still more wolf than human as he stared at me. "I found you!"

Praise to the Goddess, he was a fine specimen. He was tall and dark and built like a linebacker. His dark eyes burned like coals against his tan face. A light scruff covered his square jaw and, oh crap, my kryptonite—he had a chin cleft. Yum. And he clearly had an animal side. But why was he here?

Oh! This suddenly made sense. He was just as I'd visualized when I'd done the love spell for my sister. A sense of loss rolled through me as I shook my head and pointed at Pepper.

"You're here for her, Wolfie, not me."

Pepper stepped forward, her eyes wide as she examined the wide shoulders, the hard planes of his chest, the muscled arms, and the happy trail that ran from the bottom of his eight pack abs to an erect cock that was, well, let's just say it was proportionate to the rest of him.

I tamped down the sudden jealous urge to push Pepper out of the way and block him from my sister's eager eyes. After all, she was the one who'd called for him. This man was going to be my brother-in-law. I couldn't be lusting after him, that was just gross. I stifled a sigh. Pepper had all the luck.

"It's me," Pepper confirmed, giving him a little wave. "I'm your mate. You're here for me."

The man shook his head, sparing Pepper a quick glance before his intense gaze returned to me. My entire body tingled as he looked me up and down, his gaze almost like a touch.

"Mate, I've been looking for you my whole life."

I could see the truth in his eyes. This man, this shifter, he truly believed I was his mate. I tried not to notice how warm and fuzzy that made me feel. My whole life, no one had ever chosen me. Pepper was the pretty sister, and Meri was the life of the party. Me? I was the smart nerdy sister, the quiet one who guys were mostly nice to in order to meet one of my sisters.

He's not for you, I reminded myself. *You have to fix this.*

The wolf sniffed. "You're not a shifter, mate, but I sense magic in you. Are you a fae?"

"She's a witch," Meri piped up. Her amused gaze switched between me and the stranger. "Maybe not the best one though."

Pepper finally caught up. "Wait a minute," she poked the guy in the biceps, trying to get his attention again. "You really think Chamomile here is your mate?"

The man straightened as he turned to face my sister.

"I know she is my mate, without a doubt. I live over in Greysden, about thirty minutes from here. My wolf was restless, wanting to go for a run, and directed me here. As soon as he smelled his mate," he turned his head to give me another searing gaze before directing his attention back to Pepper. "As soon as we picked up her sweet scent, I lost control of my wolf, and he brought me here. To her. She is my fated mate, the other half of my soul. My wolf knows."

Pepper threw up her hands in aggravation. "Damn it, Cami, I thought you knew how to at least do a simple spell without messing it up!"

"What spell?" the stranger asked.

"Cami did a love spell that was supposed to help me find my true love." She dragged out the word 'supposed' with a sarcastic tone. "You look like just what I asked for. But she must have fucked it up somehow, because you're focused on the wrong sister."

"She isn't the wrong sister," he corrected, his voice deep and sure. "This one is my mate. Chamomile." He tried out my name like it was foreign to him, then reached out one large hand. "I'm Stephen."

Our palms touched and I gasped as a jolt of electricity ran through my body. I had the sudden urge to climb him like a tree. Stephen's nostrils flared, telling me he could smell the rush of arousal that had dampened my panties the minute we touched. Damn shifters.

"Nice to meet you, Stephen. My friends call me Cami." My voice sounded breathy, and I cringed internally. This was just the spell. I had to remember that. I wasn't this guy's soulmate, as much as I might wish it were true. Goddess, I wished it were true. "I'm sorry, but I'm not your mate. There's been a terrible mistake."

"I'll figure out how to reverse it," I told Pepper. "I just need to figure out what went wrong with the magic, then I can fix it. I promise."

She looked disgusted. "Never mind. The dude's fixated on you now. I'm not going to be his sloppy seconds."

Pepper's voice turned sad. "It figures that this would happen to me. I guess I'll never find love. I might as well embrace my old maid status. I'm going to dye my hair grey, stop wearing underwire bras, and go buy a bunch of cats."

"But you hate cats," I protested. She was also a little too busty to eschew underwires, but I didn't want to add insult to injury.

She grabbed Meri's hand and gave her a tug, pulling her away from me and the shifter. "Come on, let's give these kids some privacy."

"Pepper..." I called after my sister, but she and Meri were already gone. Both of them could move fast when they wanted to. I sighed deeply. Damn it. I felt terrible about upsetting my sister.

"What's the matter, mate?" Stephen asked. "Are you disappointed in me for some reason?"

I looked at him, my eyes traveling from his big feet, which were somehow attractive even though I hated feet, up his muscled body, and over the handsome lines of his face. He was hot as hell, but I knew what I was feeling was just because of the spell. I'd never been attracted to a guy like this before. My type was more like blonde and lean, not dark and broad, but even still, I somehow knew deep in my soul that he was perfect for me. Except for the pesky issue of him being my sister's mate.

I patted his bare chest with my hand, then regretted it immediately as the touch of our skin made another wave of arousal flow through me so strongly my knees almost buckled.

"It's not that I'm disappointed," I reassured him. I didn't know this guy, but I still didn't want to hurt his feelings.

"I'm sure you're a great guy. And you're not hard on the eyes, that's for sure. But you're here because of a spell. I messed it up somehow; I actually summoned you here for my sister, Pepper."

He nodded. "Yeah, I got that, but you're wrong," he said with a touch of arrogance in his tone that annoyed me. "I'm a shifter, our mates are determined by the fates themselves, not some witch's silly spell. You're the one I'm supposed to be with. My finding you after you did a spell for your sister is just a coincidence."

"Magic isn't silly," I protested. "You look exactly like what my sister said she wanted."

"Do you really think the way we feel right now is only because of your magic?" he asked, stepping closer. "Do you think I can't smell that you're as attracted to me as I am to you, little mate?"

Alpha energy was coming off this guy in waves. I took a step back, suddenly nervous. He followed, eyes darkening as he stalked me like prey. I took another step, then another, until my back hit a tree. Stephen crowded up close to me, putting one hand on either side of my head, his large palms pressing into the bark. He was as close as he could be without actually touching me. The air around us was thick and felt charged. My body was vibrating with awareness, and it took every bit of my self-control to not close the distance between us.

"If it's not magic, I don't know what this is," I whispered.

"It's fate."

Stephen

The minute my lips touched Cami's I knew my wolf had been right. Cami was my fated mate. The one being in all the world who was meant just for me. Not that I doubted him, not really, but any hesitation my human side felt faded away as I kissed her.

Every cell in my body stilled and a sense of peace filled me. I'd heard my parents talk about this, the sense of rightness that a shifter felt the first time they kissed their mate. I'd disregarded their stories as romantic fantasies, but this was no fantasy. It was a dream come true.

I nipped at her bottom lip, demanding entrance into the sweet heat of her mouth. She complied, sighing as my tongue swept in and tangled with hers.

My mate was perfect. Better than I could have ever hoped for. She was on the tall side, maybe five eight to my six foot two height. She had long straight brown hair that went past her shoulders, and large brown eyes that stood in contrast to the paleness of her white face. Her features were sharp, except her mouth which looked like the cutest little red bow. She was curvy as hell, with large pendulous breast, thick thighs, and a slim waist that gently sloped into full hips. Fate had chosen well. I couldn't have described a more attractive mate even if I'd done a spell of my own.

I chuckled internally, thinking of her insistence that the attraction between us was due to some spell. I'd grown up around witches – this entire part of the state was full of magical beings, attracted by the energy vortexes that converged under the Earth in this area. One thing I knew about spells: there was always an element of choice. A person could resist a witch's spell if they were strong willed enough, but no one could resist the shifter mating call. Shifters would die rather than be away from their true mates.

She's ours, my wolf confirmed. *We must mark her and stake our claim.*

I could feel my canines pushing at my gums, my wolf eager to sink its teeth into the softness of Cami's milky white neck. But I knew instinctively that it would be a mistake to rush her. I pulled back from the kiss and stared down into my mate's beautiful face. Her eyes were glassy, and she looked a little dazed. I felt a sense of pride that I'd affected her like that. She wasn't the only one who felt off-kilter.

"I want nothing more than to take you against this tree and make you mine," I started. My cock twitched as the sweet scent of her increased arousal hit my nostrils. "But I think you need time to adjust to the news of us finding each other."

Cami straightened, her eyes clearing as the haze of attraction ebbed. "Look Wolfie, I don't want a mate, and even if I did, I can't do this to my sister. I won't hurt her like this. Sisters before Misters, that's been our sacred vow since we grew breasts."

She placed a hand on my chest, her palm searing me like a brand. I let her push me away, even as my wolf whined deep inside me. *Be patient,* I chastised him. He wasn't the most patient animal.

"I'm sorry, but I've got to get home and figure out how to fix this spell."

"Do you really want me to be with your sister?" I asked curiously. "You want me to kiss her the way I just kissed you?"

Her eyes blazed with anger before she tamped it down again. Her reaction gave me comfort.

"You don't understand. She put an intention out to the universe, asking for her perfect man. She described you in great detail and you're just as she described. The perfect man for her."

"I'm the perfect man for you Cami." Her eyes flew to mine as I pressed on. "And you're the perfect woman for me. Not your sister. You."

"You don't even know me," she argued. "It's best if we just say goodbye."

"I don't need to know you. My wolf knows you. And we're not going to give you up without a fight Cami. I need you. And I think you need me too."

She was shaking her head before I even finished. "No. This can't happen. I need to go."

"Play with your potions as much as you want, little witch. That won't change anything. I've got fate on my side."

I stalked over and kissed her softly on the forehead. "I'll come see you tomorrow."

"You mean you'll come see Pepper."

I shook my head. "I said exactly what I mean. Until tomorrow, mate."

"You don't even know where I live," she said confidently.

I tapped the side of my nose. "I don't need to know, my wolf will sniff you out."

She rolled her eyes. "Damn shifters."

With one last look at my mate, I stepped back and inhaled deeply, calling my wolf forward. The air around me shifted and I felt the familiar sensation of my bones breaking and lengthening, muscles expanding, claws and fangs extending. Dark fur pushed through my pores, and I dropped to all fours.

When the change was complete, I padded over to my mate, who stood watching nearby. I nudged her with my head, and she leaned down to stroke the fur between my ears. My wolf preened happily.

"Bye Wolfie," she whispered sadly.

I held my wolf back as she hurried away, assuring him that we would find her again tomorrow. Maybe by then she'd have had enough time to accept our pairing. Connecting with a fated mate was always easier when both parties were shifters, but I was confident she would come around.

I ambled back through the woods, heading to where I'd parked my car. The ground was soft underneath my paws due a recent rainstorm, and my wolf inhaled the fresh damp air as I continued on my journey. I loved this part of being a shifter. Being one with the forest, hearing the animals skittering around as they sensed my approach, smelling all the scents of growth and decay that I couldn't detect when I was in my human form. It felt so freeing to run like this. But no run had ever been so joyous.

I'd finally found my mate. I had turned forty a few months ago, and after so many years alone I had started to worry that I'd never have a mate. My siblings had settled down with their mates, embarking on long happy marriages just like our parents had. Mom and Dad had been mates for fifty years and married for nearly as long. We were planning their fiftieth anniversary party later this year, and I couldn't wait to celebrate with my mate by my side.

I just needed to get her off this idea that her spell had gone wrong and that I was intended for her sister. Either her spell hadn't worked, or it had worked but the sister's mate hadn't found her yet. Either way, it was an unfortunate coincidence that I'd found her right after she'd tried to help her sister. I wasn't going to let that stop me though. I wanted to spend the rest of my life with my mate, and I was eager for the rest of my life to start right away.

Besides, if Pepper was a decent woman, she would want her sister to be happy. And she wouldn't want me to be with her when she knew my heart belonged to Cami.

I'd find Cami tomorrow and talk some sense into her. If all else failed, I could just throw her over my shoulder, bring her back to my den, and kiss her until she realized the truth. Cami was mine.

Cami

As soon as I got back to the Rosewater Mansion, I started looking for Pepper. I found her in the library, thumbing through an old photo album with a sad expression on her face. She looked like she'd lost her best friend – or her mate. My heart pinched at her sadness.

"Hey," I said, coming to sit in the chair across from her. "I'm so so sorry Pepper. I don't know what happened. I swear I was only focused on you during the spell. You know that I don't even want a mate."

"No, but your mate wants you," she said sadly. "I'm not mad at you Cami, if that's what you're worried about. I know you did your best, and I want you to be happy as much as I want that for myself. If that wolf makes you happy, then so be it. I wish you both the best, truly."

I shook my head. "No, I'm going to figure out how to reverse the spell and we can do it again."

"No, that's not necessary. I was talking to Meri, and she said something that made a lot of sense. A love spell is too personal to put in someone else's hands, even if that someone else is as close as we are. That's what went wrong with the spell. I should have done it myself, if only I had some power."

It was a source of ongoing frustration for Pepper that I'd inherited some of Mom's magic, and Meri had some of Dad's psychic abilities, glitchy as they both were, but Pepper was just a regular human with no supernatural talent at all. Or if she had some, it had never manifested.

I sighed deeply. "I wish Mom was here, she would have known how to do the spell properly."

A flush rose up Pepper's face. "Um. Well, the thing is, I asked Mom first."

"What?"

"I asked her last time she was in town to do a love spell for me, and she refused. She said it was a terrible idea. She said that I couldn't rush fate and that the universe would bring me someone in good time if I was just patient and made myself open to the possibilities."

I felt a wave of irritation. "Mom said it was a bad idea, so you asked me? Even knowing that my powers are sporadic and quirky?"

She nodded. "Yeah, I figured it was either try it with you or visit a sperm bank. I guess I'll be visiting a sperm bank."

"Peppermint Mugwort Rosewater, you are NOT going to a sperm bank!"

My sister grimaced at my use of her full name. None of us sisters were particularly fond of our weird names.

"I can if I want to, Chamomile Ginseng Rosewater, you're not the boss of me."

I rolled my eyes at her childish retort. "How do you think your soulmate will feel when he finds you and you're walking around with some anonymous guy's kid?"

"I really don't care how some imaginary guy that I may or may not ever meet would feel. This is about me. It's my life, and I've wanted to be a mother since I was five years old. I'm sick of waiting to have a family. You were my last hope."

I moved towards her and leaned down to give her a hug. "You can be your own hope, Pepper. Someone is out there for you, someone perfect, and you'll find each other soon. I just know it."

Pepper hugged me back. "Thanks Sis, I hope you're right. So, what are you going to do about your new mate?"

"Nothing." I felt a stab of pain behind my sternum as I spoke. "I'm not going to see him again. I told him it was all a mistake, and that I didn't want a mate, not now, not ever."

"How did that go?" she asked, her voice amused.

I kneeled on the floor in front of her chair and met her gaze. "He kissed me."

I could feel redness climbing up my neck and cursed my fair complexion. Kissed seemed like an understatement. It was more like a claiming. He'd ravished me with his mouth, and I'd loved every minute of it. But there was no way I was going into that with my sister. I could hardly admit it to myself.

"How was it?"

"Really good," I admitted sheepishly. "He's hot as hell, obviously, but I'd never do anything to hurt you, Pepper. You're my sister, and that's way more important than any boy."

"That boy is all man. My Goddess, did you see his giant..."

She broke off laughing as I smacked her arm. "Hey!"

Pepper leaned forward and grasped my face between her palms. "I want you to be happy as much as you want the same for me, Chamomile. You should go for it with your wolf. You have my blessing."

I shook my head. "I'm not even sure if I'll see him again, besides, you know I like being single."

"You don't know a lot about shifter mates, do you? There's no way that guy is going to stay away if you're really his mate. You'd better buckle up big sister, because I think you're in for the ride of your life."

I spent a restless night thinking about Stephen and wondering if I really was going to see him again. I hadn't been lying; I didn't want a mate. Sure, I enjoyed sex as much as the next girl, but having the same guy around day in and day out? Relying on someone else for your happiness? There was no way that I wanted that for myself. My parents were happily married, but I'd never really wanted that life, especially after my bad experience with an ex-boyfriend. I was content to be the cool weird aunt for Meri and Pepper's kids. Or I would be if either of them ever fell in love and had a family. I just wished I knew what I'd done wrong with that spell to make it backfire.

The next day the wooing started. I woke up to flowers being delivered to my house. A ridiculously large arrangement with a sweet card saying, *Beautiful flowers for my beautiful mate. Can I take you to dinner tonight?* The card included his phone number. I threw it in the trash but kept the flowers. I wasn't a total monster.

Meri texted me later that day. I was at work when Stephen showed up at the house at dinner time asking to see me. He tried to charm her out of my phone number, but my baby sister held firm. The following day more flowers came, followed by a life-sized stuffed wolf with a bow around its neck, and a few hours later, a giant box of candy. Each gift came with an entreaty to call him, which I ignored. Maybe he'd get the message that I wasn't interested. Meanwhile my sisters were pressing me to give him a chance, much to my annoyance.

On the third day I was working at the store as usual. Early on in their marriage, my parents had opened a combination bookstore, magic shop, and café called Rosewater's Magical Emporium. We'd all worked there growing up, but neither Pepper nor Meri really loved it the way I did. They helped out when needed, but they didn't have any interest in working there on a daily basis. Not like me. Rosewater's was my life.

I had studied business administration in college and after graduation I'd dedicated myself to learning all aspects of the business from Mom and Dad, working my way up from stocking shelves to being the store manager. I'd saved my money and was able to buy them out when they'd finally retired last year. Under my leadership the last thirteen years, the shop had grown and expanded into a neighboring shop, developed a social media following, and created an online store that now had better sales than our bricks and mortar store. I was proud of all my accomplishments.

The bell rang over the door just after five o'clock, and I stuck my head out in the aisle from where I was stocking shelves. I'd sent my staff person on their dinner break, so I was the only person working in the store right now besides the high school girl who was working in the back of the store at the café.

"Welcome to Rosewater's. How may I..."

I froze as a hulking figure came around a display, and my stomach dropped. It was Stephen, looking yummy as hell in faded jeans that lovingly hugged his muscular thighs, and a plain grey t-shirt that stretched tight against his enormous biceps. My mouth was immediately dry.

"Mate." His growl seemed to carry across the store as his eyes raked over me, taking in my long black knit skirt, dark pink scoop neck t-shirt, and beaded jewelry. My nipples immediately hardened, and his eyes dropped, telling me that my reaction was visible beneath the thin fabric of my shirt and bra.

"Um. Hi. How may I help you?" I asked. "We're having a sale on cozy mysteries if you're interested."

"Do you work here?" he asked, noting the opened box of books at my feet.

I nodded. "I own this shop," I told him with pride in my voice. "This section is books, and that side is for metaphysical items like crystals, tarot cards, and magical supplies. There's also a café in the back if you'd like a coffee while you shop."

"I didn't come here to shop," he told me. "I came to see my mate."

I ignored the thrill I felt at his words. "How did you find me?"

He pressed one finger against the side of his nose like he had done the other day. Damn, he wasn't kidding about being able to track me by scent. It was a little weird to think that was possible. It's not like I didn't shower. I leaned into my irritation and stepped closer, close enough that I could see his eyes glowing with his wolf.

"Maybe I wasn't clear the other day, but I summoned you by accident. It's my sister who's looking for a mate, not me. I'm not interested." I pointed in the direction of the door. "You should go now."

"Maybe I wasn't clear," he said, repeating my words. "I am not under the influence of some spell. You are my mate. Only you. My arrival after you did your little spell was just a coincidence."

He stepped closer and I stepped back, waving my hand at him, and muttering a magic incantation. A puff of smoke rose between us, then disappeared into vapor. Damn my glitchy magic. I meant to put up a force field between us to keep him away.

He raised one dark eyebrow. "That the best you can do?"

"I never said I was good at being a witch," I replied defensively.

He reached a hand out and cupped my cheek. Instinctively I leaned into his touch. It felt so...right. "I'd like to spend some time with you, Mate, so we can get to know each other better before I claim you."

"I don't think that's a good idea," I protested, even though I didn't sound particularly convincing. I hoped he couldn't smell the rush of arousal that flooded my core at his words.

"What time do you get off work?" he asked. I tried to be annoyed that he was ignoring me, but somehow, I couldn't. A small part of me appreciated his single-minded focus on me, even though I would never admit that.

"I'm working until closing time," I responded. "Maybe I'll see you some other time."

"I'll just grab a cup of coffee and wait until you're done then."

"But..."

"You said the café is back here?" he said, walking backwards and pointing in the direction of the café.

"But..."

"Just let me know when you're ready to go."

"But..."

He disappeared around the corner of the shelves as I stared after him with my mouth open.

"You might as well give up. You summoned a stubborn one." I jumped as I heard Meri's amused voice behind me.

"Meri! I didn't hear you come in!"

My youngest sister laughed. "Yeah, you didn't even twitch when the bell over the door rang. You were a little busy with your new boyfriend."

I stared at her. Over the years I'd become so conditioned to hear that bell over the door that I was like one of Pavlov's dogs. I heard the bell when I was back in my office. I heard the bell in the alley when I was taking out the trash. I even heard it in my sleep. I never missed the bell. I couldn't believe that damn wolf had distracted me so much.

Meri put her hands on her hips. "So, what's your beef with the big guy?" she asked, nodding in the direction that Stephen had gone. I'd ignored that same question from her for the last two days, but this time I answered.

"First of all, I did a spell to find the perfect mate for Pepper, not for myself."

"Pepper doesn't care about that, and I know she's told you that. It was a stupid idea anyway, both of you should have known it wasn't going to work."

"Second," I continued as if she hadn't spoken. "I don't want a mate."

"Yeah, I could see why you wouldn't want a big hulky guy who fate ordained is perfect for you," she said, her voice laden with sarcasm. "Why would you want someone who will be physically incapable of abandoning you or cheating on you. Someone who will protect you and never hurt you. I mean, my Goddess, who would want that?"

"Third," I pressed on. "I like my life the way it is right now. I have no time for a boyfriend, let alone a mate."

My sister rolled her eyes. "Well, I don't know why fate is wasting a perfectly good mate on someone like you, Chamomile. I mean sure, both Pepper and I would die to have someone to love us, but instead the perfect man goes to the one sister who won't appreciate it."

"Are you done being dramatic?" I asked.

She nodded.

"Can you finish my shift for me?" I asked. "I can tell this guy's not going to leave me alone until I go out with him and talk some sense into him." Ignoring him wasn't helping, so I figured I'd go grab a drink with him or something so he could see for himself what a terrible match we were.

"Sure Sis, I'll finish your shift for you, don't worry. You go hang out with your looove." Meri drew out the last work teasingly.

Before I could snap back a retort there was a blur and a rush of air, and then Stephen was in front of me. "What the...?"

"I heard you're free now," he told me. "Let's go."

Before I could respond I was lifted into the air and was thrown across one muscular shoulder like a sack of flour. I stared at his broad back in shock, then punched him in the kidney as hard as I could.

"Hey! Put me down asshole!"

He grunted as my blow hit, but only clamped his arm tight around the back of my thighs, holding me close to him. My entire body was on fire from touching him, and my mind was too jumbled to think of a spell to help me get free.

Meanwhile Meri was cracking up like it was the funniest thing she'd ever seen. "I think you've met your match Chamomile. You kids have fun now."

Stephen

Was it wrong of me to practically kidnap my mate? Maybe. But I couldn't find it in me to care. Clearly at least one of her sisters were on my side, and I hoped that would make it easier for me to convince my mate that it was fate that brought us together, not witchcraft. If not, I would just have to tie her to my bed until she saw reason. My wolf rumbled in agreement.

"Where are you taking me?" she asked, wiggling like a fish on a hook and kicking hard against my grip. I could feel the anger rolling off her as she nailed me in the gut with the tip of one shoe. "Let me go right now!"

"Quiet!" I smacked her plump ass in response. She gasped in outrage even while I smelled her arousal. Interesting. My cock twitched in response.

I carried her to my SUV that was parked in the lot near the store. "We're going to my place so we can talk in private," I told her as I unlocked the passenger side door. "Will you sit still, or do I need to get the rope from the trunk?"

Another gasp of outrage. "Fine. Whatever." Her tone was sullen as she sagged back against the seat and crossed her arms.

"Great. Buckle up, Mate. And if you're thinking of running, I'd like to remind you that I have something you don't have."

I paused dramatically and she raised one eyebrow.

"Superhuman speed."

She rolled her eyes. I quickly closed her door and jogged around to the driver's side, turning on the car and backing out of my parking spot before she could get any more crazy ideas. She was mostly silent on the twenty minute drive to my house, other than a few dramatic sighs. I didn't bother trying to make conversation. I figured it was useless until she calmed down. I knew my actions were heavy-handed, but after a couple of days apart I was desperate to be close to her. Sending her gifts didn't work, so kidnapping her seemed like the next logical step to my lust-addled mind.

I owned a house on the outskirts of a town called Greysden. It was a shifter town, originally founded by grey wolves, but over the years the community had welcomed all manner of shifters from lions to bears to badgers. We even had some bunny shifters. Unlike a lot of shifter towns, there was no ruling alpha or rules about moving in. It was truly a mixed community where everyone was welcome, even the humans who mostly pretended that shifters didn't exist.

I pulled into my driveway and hit the garage door opener. Once I'd safely parked my SUV in the garage, I turned off the engine and went around to open her door. Cami ignored my hand and slid out of the vehicle with a glare that made my cock twitch again. I loved how strong and fiery she was.

I gestured for her to go ahead of me, and she entered the side door into the house. She looked around curiously, taking in the overstuffed dark blue furniture and earth tones on the walls. My place was clean and comfortable, if a bit understated. Cami wandered over to the fireplace and looked at the pictures on the mantle.

"My family," I explained as she picked one photo up to look at it more carefully. "You'll meet them soon. Everyone was very excited when I told them about you." I had a big family with three siblings and a bunch of cousins.

"I agreed to one date, and that's it," she snipped. Her face was flushed and damn if her pissed off face wasn't turning me on. I loved that my mate was a strong woman, and I wasn't afraid to work a little to get her affection.

"Actually, you didn't agree to anything," I reminded her. "That's why I had to take drastic measures."

"All the freaking men in the world and I get this guy?" she mumbled. "Damn my glitchy magic."

"I heard you, and I'll just let you know that I'm a total catch. You're very lucky."

She slammed her hands onto her hips. "Who told you that? Your momma?"

"Among other people," I replied mildly. "How about a drink?"

She sighed. "Do you have any decent beer?"

I went to get us both a beer, grateful for the chance to regroup a bit. I hadn't planned to bring her back here, at least not involuntarily, and I wasn't totally sure what my next move should be. I handed her a beer and nodded at the couch.

"Shall we get to know each other a little bit?"

She sat down without a word.

"Tell me about yourself," I invited. I knew that women usually liked to talk about themselves. I figured if I could get her to open up a bit, she would see how perfect we were for each other.

"Hmm, well, let's see. I like being single, and I don't want to get married or have kids. I like being independent, and I hate being manhandled."

I burst out laughing. "It's funny, but I can tell that even you don't believe what you're saying. Even without wolf's sense of smell I could have scented your arousal when I threw you over my shoulder and smacked your sweet ass."

Cami popped out of her seat. "You're such an asshole."

I stood up and stepped in front of her. "I'm your asshole now."

Before she could respond, I slid my hand behind her head and crashed my lips to hers. I swallowed her gasp and deepened the kiss, pulling her closer to me. I loved the feeling of Cami melting against me as her resistance faded. Her arms slid around my waist, sliding under the hem of my t-shirt to grip the muscles of my lower back.

I took a few steps backwards until the back of my knees hit the couch, then sat down, pulling her on top of me. I readjusted her so that she was straddling me, all without breaking the kiss. At this point I was hard as a rock and Cami was grinding her core against me like she was trying to get herself off through our clothes. I started reciting baseball stats in my head to keep myself from coming in my pants like a teenage boy.

I finally broke the kiss so we could get a breath. Kissing and nibbling down the side of her neck, I sucked on the spot where her neck met her shoulder, imagining how I could place my mark there someday soon. Her hands tightened on my shoulders, and she tilted her head to give me better access. Her breath was coming in small bursts, and I could smell how turned on she was.

My wolf was pushing on me to claim her on the spot, but I reminded him that we needed to be patient with our human mate. I really did want to get to know Cami better before we took the next step. Her stomach growled loudly, catching my attention, and I slowly pulled back to put some space between us. I didn't want to freak her out just when she was softening towards me.

"Are you hungry?"

My mate's eyes were hooded. "Yeah, I could eat." Her stomach growled again, and we both laughed.

"How about I make you dinner?" My wolf chuffed in approval that we would taking care of our mate with food.

"You can cook?" She seemed surprised.

"I have many talents." I shifted her off my lap and stood up, reaching for her hand. "Keep me company while I cook?"

I took it as a victory when she came along without an argument.

Cami

Stephen decided to grill, so we worked together to marinate the meat and prepare some vegetables to barbeque. As we prepped the food, he told me a bit about himself and as I relaxed more, I found myself sharing about myself as well. Despite my concerns about the role of magic in his attraction for me, I felt comfortable with him in a way that didn't usually happen until I'd known someone for a long time. Conversation flowed between us with surprising ease.

"What do you do for a living?" I asked.

"I work at Grey Construction," he explained. "My friend Stuart Grey is the owner. We mostly do home remodels and occasional retail interiors."

"Have you worked there long?"

"About fifteen years," he responded. "It's perfect for me, and I love the work."

"It's great when you find work that's meaningful," I responded. "Too many people I know hate their jobs."

"I know you said that you own Rosewater's." At my nod he asked, "Do you have a set schedule at the store?"

"Not really. I'm there most weekdays but I also fill in nights and weekends depending on where I have holes in the schedule."

"How many people work for you?"

"I have one other full-time person and about six part-timers. And my sisters help out when I need them to. We all grew up working in the store, so even though I'm the sole owner now, it's kind of a given that anyone else in the family will pitch in when we need them."

"It's good that you're close with your sisters. Is it just the three of you?"

I nodded and shared that my parents were currently traveling the world but when they were in town, they stayed at the family home. I followed Stephen out to the deck and held the platter of food while he opened the grill and laid out some charcoal. He opened a can of lighter fluid, and I stopped him with a hand on his arm.

"That stuff's toxic," I admonished. "Step back."

He followed my instructions with a curious look. Handing him the platter, I moved closer to the grill and waved my finger towards the charcoal. "*Incindre.*" The charcoal immediately lit up. At least my magic was good enough to start a fire, I thought wryly.

"Nice trick," Stephen told me, leaning forward to plant a quick kiss on the tip of my nose. "Now move away and let the man grill our meat."

I rolled my eyes at his teasing. "Yeah OK, I'll just sit here and enjoy my beer then, grill man."

I watched him as he grilled some ground beef patties and vegetables. He moved with a quiet grace that really appealed to me. It made me wonder about his prowess with other types of activities. Suddenly Stephen's head shot up and he met my eyes, as if he could read my mind. Maybe he could, at least a little bit. I'd read that when a shifter was around their fated mate, a bond formed between them that allowed them to tune into each other's emotions. We hadn't slept together, nor had he marked me, but I could still feel the first tenuous strands of a connection between us. I wondered if it felt stronger to him, since he was a shifter.

We ate dinner on the deck, sitting across from each other at a picnic table situated at one end. The sun was starting to fade as we finished our meal. I couldn't deny that I enjoyed hanging out with Stephen, much more than I'd expected. I'd been so focused on the spell that went sideways that I hadn't really allowed myself to wonder who this man really was. He definitely seemed like a good one. I studied him covertly across the table. His scruff was darker now, almost hiding that cute little dimple in his chin. It made him look a little dangerous.

I licked my lips and heard him groan. In a flash he was on his feet and around the table, dropping on the bench next to me. It never ceased to amaze me how quickly these shifters could move.

"What...?"

I didn't get to finish my sentence before Stephen lowered his head and caught my lips with his. His fingers threaded through my long hair, holding my head in place as he nipped at my lower lip, demanding entrance to my mouth. I opened with a sigh. How could I not? The minute his lips touched mine, everything in my body simultaneously lit up and settled down. It was the strangest feeling.

Stephen's other hand slid down to cup one breast, squeezing it gently. I moaned into his mouth as my nipple hardened painfully. My own hands started traveling, sneaking beneath his tight t-shirt to explore the hard planes of his chest. I was starting to see the appeal of a big, burly guy.

I slid my hand down his stomach until I was able to cup the hard erection that was pressing against his jeans. I'd seen it before, of course, it was on full display the other day when we were in the woods, but having his thickness in the palm of my hand really drove the point home, so to speak, that this was a big guy. I couldn't wait to feel him stretching my channel. That's when I made a decision. It had been way too long since I'd been attracted to a man, and honestly, I missed sex. I pulled away and Stephen looked at me curiously.

"I want you," I told him. "But I need to be clear that that I don't want anything serious. If we do this, it's only for tonight. I don't want a mate."

His eyes darkened then glimmered with the hint of his wolf. "We can talk about the mate thing later," he said, jumping off the bench and pulling me to my feet. "For now, I want dessert."

With one sweep of his long arm, he sent everything on the table crashing to the deck. Plates, bottles, leftovers...it all went flying. Before I could take my next breath, Stephen grabbed me by the waist and lifted me up to lay flat on the table. My heart was racing, and my panties were soaked. Wait, what had I been talking to him about?

I raised to my elbows. "What are you doing?"

"I can't wait another moment to taste you," he growled. Stephen gripped the elastic waistband of my skirt and ripped it down my legs, taking my panties with it and leaving me bare. He tossed my clothes over his shoulder and stared down at my glistening pussy with a look that was pure desire.

I felt a thrill. Never in my life had anyone been so overcome with passion for me like this. I'd had relationships of course, and I'd always enjoyed sex, but this felt very different. Before I could think about why that was, Stephen dropped to his knees, pulled my ass closer to the edge of the table, and threw my legs over his shoulders. Thank the Goddess the table was sealed wood, or I would have gotten a very unfortunate splinter in my ass.

Stephen growled something that sounded suspiciously like "Mine!" before lowering his head. His rough tongue slid through my wet folds, lapping up my essence and building my excitement. I shuddered as he licked up and down a few times before turning his full attention to my throbbing clit.

Stephen tapped his tongue against the sensitive bundle of nerves, then circled a few times before resuming the tapping motion. I gasped as he inserted one thick finger into my channel, slowly pumping in and out. I rolled my head from side to side, rocking my hips against his face to encourage him to get closer to where I needed him. I heard him chuckle against me. He slipped a second finger inside me, curling his fingers to find my G-spot. At the same time, he lowered his head and sucked my clit between his lips. That was all it took for me to come completely undone. I trembled under the force of my orgasm, clamping my thighs tighter against his head and gasping as wave after wave of pleasure shook my body.

"Fuck," I gasped as I came down from the waves of pleasure.

Stephen's head popped up, licking his lips. "Mmm. Delicious."

I felt a wave of heat rise up my face. I enjoyed oral as much as the next girl, but I'd never been so shameless, never come so loudly and quickly. What had gotten into me?

"Oh no." Stephen pushed to his feet and slid me farther up the picnic table before crawling up to trap me under his bulky body. He pushed up on his elbows so he could look down at me.

"Oh no?" I asked in confusion. "What?"

"Don't start thinking," he commanded, his voice a deep growl.

"Um…"

"I want you so bad Cami," he interrupted. "Please don't make me wait any longer."

I couldn't help but giggle. "Longer?" I asked. "We've known each other for like forty-eight hours."

"That's forever to a shifter who's found his mate," he said solemnly.

"What are you waiting for then?" I asked softly. "Take me."

His eyes widened, then he slid off the table, shucked his pants, and before I knew what was happening, he was back between my legs, notching his thick cock between my folds.

"Are you sure?" he asked. I could see a hint of his canines lengthening with excitement.

I nodded. "Just don't bite me, Wolfie. I meant it when I said this was only for one night."

Stephen slid into me in one long, hard thrust, making us both gasp. I felt so full I could hardly breathe. He leaned down, kissing me deeply as he gave me some time to adjust. The minute the grip of my internal muscles relaxed, he started moving, sliding in and out in a rhythm that I quickly matched. I wrapped my legs around his waist, tilting my pelvis and pulling him deeper.

"You feel so good, Mate," he ground out. "I can't believe we finally found each other."

I slid my hands up beneath the shirt he was still wearing, and ran my nails up his strong back, scoring the skin. He hissed at the sensation, picking up the pace. There was nothing tentative in his movements, like there often was when you were with someone for the first time. With every thrust Stephen pushed so deep inside me that it was impossible to know where he ended and I started. It was heavenly. I could feel my body tightening as another orgasm crashed down on me.

"Stephen!" I gasped.

He lowered his head to the crook of my neck, pounding into me for all he was worth. As my inner muscles squeezed around him, he let himself go, coming with a long groan of masculine satisfaction. I felt the heat of his cum filling me up before he collapsed on top of me, panting harshly against my shoulder. I shivered beneath him. We stayed still for a long time. I thought he might have fallen asleep, but he finally lifted his head and pressed a soft kiss against my lips.

"That was incredible Mate, but we still have a lot of night left."

Stephen

When I dropped Cami off at her house the next morning, I could swear she was walking funny. And why wouldn't she? We'd made love so many times last night I'd lost count. We'd barely gotten any sleep at all, and I knew that a full day of manual labor today was going to be challenging. Cami wasn't the only one with sore muscles this morning, but it had definitely been worth it.

I'd made good progress with my mate last night and although she still didn't want me to mark her, I knew she was softening to me. And not just because I gave her about a dozen orgasms. It was the connection we'd felt, the way we'd talked softly as we rested between rounds of lovemaking. In the darkness of night, we'd both opened up to each other, talking until we could barely stay awake.

Don't get me wrong, it had been a struggle holding my wolf back from marking her and claiming her in the way only a shifter could. But he'd been comforted by spending the night together and feeling the mate bond growing stronger between us even without my marking her.

I'd been expecting Cami to pull away in the morning but while she'd been pretty quiet on the ride over to her house, she hadn't totally withdrawn. I called that a win, even though she refused to commit to getting together again.

"Remember what I said? One night only Stephen."

Her words had lacked conviction though. I'd walked her to her door and kissed her senseless on the porch, feeling a surge of masculine pride when she stumbled into her house looking dazed.

I rolled into work with a satisfied smile on my face. My boss Stuart immediately noticed my unusually cheerful demeanor.

"What happened?" he asked suspiciously. "It's not like you to be so happy in the morning."

It was true. I was not a morning person. If I didn't have to work, I would stay up late and sleep in every morning.

"I found my mate," I told him proudly.

He raised his eyebrows. "Wow, that's great man. Congratulations. Tell me about her while we lay the kitchen tile."

I told Stuart the whole story as we worked side by side. We'd been friends for a long time, and I knew that he'd had some challenges convincing his mate Kat to accept him as her mate. Even though she was a tiger shifter and understood all about fated mates, she and Stuart had a bit of a bumpy road to their happily ever after.

"She thinks a shifter would fall under a love spell?" he snorted. "We're stronger minded than that."

"It doesn't matter, it's what she believes," I explained.

"Well, you'll just have to change her mind." He shot me a smirk. "Lots of orgasms are effective."

I rolled my eyes. "I already gave her that last night, but there's still a wall between us. And when I suggested getting together again tonight, she told me that she was too busy to date anyone. She said even though last night was quote 'fun', she didn't want to see me again."

That part stung, I had to admit, even though when Cami said it, she seemed to be trying to convince herself as much as me.

"Well, you'll just need to break those walls down," Stuart told me, as if it was the easiest thing in the world.

"How?"

"Start by seeing if you can get her family and friends on your side."

I thought about Stuart's words for the rest of the morning. On my lunch break I poked around on social media until I found Cami's sister Pepper. Given that she was the one Cami was most worried about, I wanted to see if I could get her on my side. I sent her a message asking to meet and, to my surprise, she agreed. She didn't want to meet in their town in case we ran into Cami, so we agreed to get a drink at Murphy's Bar here in Greysden.

Pepper was already sitting at one of the high tops when I got there. I greeted our waitress Marie and ordered a beer. Murphy's Bar was an institution in this town, and the wolf shifter had worked here at Murphy's since she was in high school. We'd all thought she would leave town when the original owner, Murph, died, but then his son Ben had inherited the bar. To everyone's surprise, the bear shifter from New York City was her mate. Like so many of my friends, they'd had a bit of a rocky road to happily ever after, but they now appeared to be blissfully happy. The sassy wolf and serious bear made a great couple.

"What did you want to talk to me about?" Pepper asked, sucking on a straw dipped into what looked like some kind of fruity blended drink. She seemed friendly, not at all upset about what happened with the spell, so I took that as a good sign.

"I need your help."

Pepper shot me an amused look. "Ah yeah, I suspected that was it. Cami giving you some trouble?"

I nodded. "I mean, we had a great night together last night..."

"Yeah Meri told me that you carried Cami out of the store yesterday like a caveman," she laughed. "Given that she didn't come home until this morning, we figured things had gone well."

"They did go well, but she's still resistant to the idea of being mates. I know part of it is that she thinks you're mad about her messing up the spell, but it feels like more than that."

Pepper nodded. "Yeah, my sister is a stubborn one, and she's always said she wanted to be single. Even when she was a kid. But I think you'll win her over if you're patient. I know that's not in your shifter DNA, but she's going to need time to get used to the idea of being mates. Don't worry though, Meri and I are in your corner. We've talked about this, and we both agree that we just want our sister to be happy, and we think she'll be happy with you. We'll do whatever we can to make that happen."

She took another long draw of her drink. "Just promise me you'll treat her right. She's had some asshole boyfriends in the past."

My wolf growled deep inside at the idea of someone hurting our mate. Or touching her. I knew going into last night that she wasn't a virgin or anything – she was in her late thirties after all—but it was best if I didn't think about the guys who came before me.

"I'll treat her like the princess she is," I vowed.

Cami's sister snorted. "Yeah, princess, that describes my sister. Did you guys make plans to see each other again?"

I shook my head and glumly took a sip of my beer. "No, I couldn't pin her down on getting together again. She says she's too busy for me."

"Well, if she's going to be stubborn, you're just going to need to be a stray cat."

"Stray cat?"

"You know how stray cats come around and then if you feed them, they keep coming around and the next thing you know, you kind of have a cat even though you really didn't want one?"

"No, not really. I'm a wolf, remember? Cats don't really like our kind."

Pepper sighed deeply and muttered something under her breath that sounded like, *idiot men.*

"What I mean is, you need to keep showing up wherever she is, insinuating yourself into her life until she can't remember not having you there. And turn up the smolder." She looked at me critically. "You're a charming enough guy, make her swoon."

"Swoon?" I asked in confusion.

Pepper sighed again. "Build up the tension. Stay close to her. Give her a lot of innocent touches, or maybe flirt with another woman and make her jealous, that kind of thing. Be charming and flirty and stay in her orbit, and you'll make her go crazy wanting you. But don't put out again without a commitment."

"Are you saying I should withhold sex?"

"You need to do whatever it takes to make her so desperate that she'll agree to be your mate."

I frowned, feeling slightly insulted. "Are you saying she would have to be desperate to be with me?"

Pepper waved at Marie. "Good Goddess, I'm going to need another drink. You're even more hopeless than I thought."

Cami

The door to the shop opened just before closing time. I wasn't surprised to see it was Stephen. I didn't need to be my psychic sister to figure out he'd turn up eventually. Not that I could blame him. Last night had been phenomenal. I could have happily stayed in bed with Stephen until we both died of hunger. He was that good.

But once I'd gotten away from the overwhelming pull of hormones, I'd realized what a huge mistake it had been to sleep with him. It was going to be way harder to keep him at a distance now that I knew how explosive things were between us. *You agreed to one night only,* I reminded myself.

"Mate." He pulled me into a long hug. I breathed in his scent and allowed myself to relax into him for a long moment before pulling away. Damn he smelled good. This close to him, I had a hard time remembering why I was supposed to be avoiding him.

"What are you doing here?" I asked, forcing myself to sound irate even though part of me was happy to see him. "I told you I wasn't free tonight." I'd lied, but he didn't need to know that.

"I'm just looking for a book."

"What kind of book?" I asked suspiciously.

"How to please a woman."

I choked on my own spit. "I think you could probably write that book."

He gave me a sexy smirk. "It never hurts to study up on new techniques."

I sighed. "Look in aisle five."

To my surprise he ambled off to find a book instead of staying near me. Hmm, maybe he'd finally gotten the message that I wasn't interested. I continued working, one eye on Stephen the whole time. He was acting like just another guy looking for a book. That was weird. I had just made the announcement that the store was closing when he came up to the counter with several books.

"Find what you need?" I asked in my professional voice.

He looked amused, but just said, "Yes thank you."

I rang up his books. "That'll be thirty-four twenty-three."

He handed me his credit card, his hand brushing against mine just a moment too long. I swear it was enough for me to dampen my panties. What was it about this guy? I'd never been this horny in my life. I swear I wanted to throw him on the floor and ride him right here in my store. Holding myself back with effort, I finished his transaction and slid the card on the counter towards him, carefully avoiding touching him again. He grabbed his books and receipt and gave me a casual smile.

"Thanks, see you later." And then he was gone.

What the hell? What happened to the pushy shifter who'd badgered me all morning about getting together again? Had he changed his mind about me already? Maybe last night wasn't as good as I thought. I had a feeling I was going to have a long night with my vibrator after this encounter.

The next couple of days it seemed like I ran in to Stephen everywhere I went. The coffee shop. The grocery store. The gas station. I even ran into him when I was at the bank. When I saw him waiting in line at the ATM behind me, I'd had enough.

"What are you doing here?" I asked. My hands came to my hips, and I gave him my best glare.

He nodded at the debit card in his hand. "Getting some cash."

"You don't even live in this town," I reminded him. "I'm sure they have stores and banks in Greysden. Don't think I don't know what you're doing."

"What am I doing?" he asked with studied innocence.

I rolled my eyes. "You're trying to convince me to go out with you again."

"I haven't even called or texted you," he protested. "I can't help it if this is a small town."

I stepped closer and jabbed him in the chest with my finger. "Leave me alone."

He grabbed my hand and engulfed it in his much larger hand. I could feel the work-roughened skin against my softer skin, and it reminded me of how much I loved having those hands on other parts of my body. My nipples hardened and I felt a flush of arousal. When his nostrils flared and he got that irritating smirk on his face, I knew he smelled my body's reaction, which just pissed me off more. Shooting him another glare, I stalked away. I ignored the twinge in my chest as I put distance between us.

When I got home from work that, both of my sisters were there in the living room. It wasn't unheard of for the three of us to be home at the same time, we all lived together after all, but with our busy schedules, it wasn't an everyday occurrence either.

"Ah, there she is. Welcome home, big sister."

I looked at Pepper suspiciously. "What?"

She shot me an innocent look. "Nothing. Just welcoming you home Chamomile. Meri and I were thinking that we might go out for dinner or something. Do you want to join us?"

"Only if I get to pick the place."

I didn't trust my sisters not to try to manufacture some coincidental meeting with Stephen. They had both been driving me crazy all week, pushing me to give him a chance. What they didn't understand was that as much as I was tempted, I couldn't let myself get close. There was no way I was willing to let myself be vulnerable around a man. After the disastrous end of my last relationship, I'd promised myself I'd stay single. I promised myself no one would ever hurt me again.

I'd met Frank at a booksellers' conference in Denver. He was a few years older than me, tall and handsome and charming. The attraction between us was strong and immediate. We'd fallen into bed hours after we met, and we got pretty serious pretty fast. My parents still owned the store at the time, giving me a lot more free time to go on long walks and spend lazy weekend days snuggling with someone who seemed perfect for me.

The verbal abuse was subtle when it started. The off-hand comments about my weight. The "joke" that my sisters got "all the beauty" in the family and I was lucky he hadn't met one of them first. The snarky comments about nepotism, implying that I hadn't earned my position as store manager of our family business. Frank gradually chipped away at my self-esteem over the course of our time together and yet some part of me thought he was the best I could get. He acted like I should be pathetically grateful that he wanted to be with me, and gradually I started to believe it myself. My sisters both actively hated him, but I convinced myself that they were just jealous that I had someone in my life when they didn't. I should have realized that my sisters were much better than that.

I don't know how long I would have let him manipulate me, but everything came to a head one night about six months after we started dating. We had made plans for us to meet at his place, and when he wasn't there at the appointed time, I let myself in with my key. When he didn't show up, I texted and called him, worried that he'd been in a car accident or something. He'd finally come home several hours later, super drunk and belligerent. He was upset because he'd lost his job as a regional manager for a large retail bookstore chain because he hadn't been meeting his sales goals.

I knew enough about his work ethic to understand that his employer had found out about his long lunches and frequent absences, but somehow Frank decided it was my fault.

"You made me lose my job," he'd raged at me as soon as he returned home.

"Me? How would I do that?" I'd protested.

"You're too needy. Too distracting. I'm so busy dealing with you and all your neuroses that I can't concentrate on my job. You've always been jealous that I have a better job than you, one I actually earned instead of getting it from Mommy and Daddy."

I couldn't believe it. Not only were his words mean, but they were also completely untrue. He'd complained many times over the course of our relationship that I didn't have enough time for him. He resented any time I spent with family and friends. I'd finally had enough, and I spoke up to him for the first time in our relationship.

"Oh no," I'd yelled back. "You don't get to put all that on me. If you lost your job, it's because of your poor performance, not because of me."

That's when he hit me, right in the face. As I'd stumbled back and hit the wall, I couldn't believe it. I'd never been struck in my life before, other than the silly little slap fights my sisters and I had when we were younger and would get upset with each other.

I'd been filled with rage, a rage so strong that it focused my magic in a way that had never happened before. As Frank advanced on me, presumably to hit me again, I'd waved my hand and used my magic to fling him back through the air. He'd landed on the floor with a grunt, shock clearly etched on his face.

"What the fuck?"

One thing I'd never shared with Frank: that I was a witch. He started to get up, and I used the force of my magic to pin him to the floor, where he wiggled like a bug who couldn't turn over. I sent a prayer of thanks to the Goddess that my magic was working when I really needed it.

"Who the hell are you?"

"The woman who is done with you." I'd hissed. "Don't ever come near me again, or I'll make you regret it."

It had taken everything in me not to kick him as I walked by him, still pinned to the floor by my magic.

"Baby, wait," he'd whined. "I didn't mean to hurt you, I'm just so upset about my job."

I didn't even answer him as I ran out of his house for the last time. He'd badgered me for months, calling and texting and sending gifts and showing up at work. The more I resisted him, the more persistent he became. It was Meri who finally got rid of him for good. She'd came home while he was pounding on the front door, screaming for me to come outside and talk to him. Frank had turned around to try to charm her when she suddenly got one of her psychic flashes. Grabbing her head with one hand, she clutched his arm with her other.

"Miguel is coming for you," she'd intoned, her voice strong and clear. "He's angry. He wants his money for the drugs you stole from him. He's on his way."

For once, Meri's psychic abilities had worked in our favor. I'd had no idea that he was doing drugs, but Frank had turned so white at her words I could see it from the front window. Giving Meri a panicked look, he'd pulled away from her and ran to his car. That was the last we'd seen of him.

I didn't think that Stephen would behave like Frank. He was the complete opposite of him in many ways. Yet I still couldn't trust whatever was happening between us. I needed to stay away from him no matter how much I yearned to be close to him. I had learned the hard way that I could only rely on myself. No matter how compelling the wolf shifter was, I needed to stay strong.

Stephen

I hadn't seen my mate in two days, and it was making my wolf edgy. I couldn't eat, I couldn't sleep, and I couldn't stop thinking about Cami. We'd been short-handed at work, and I'd wound up putting in two consecutive twelve-hour days to help us keep on schedule. I'd scarcely had time to do more than work and sleep. Normally I didn't mind helping out and working extra hours, but knowing that my mate was out there in world unclaimed was driving my wolf crazy.

I debated heading over to see if I could find her in town but decided to wait until the next day. It was Friday night, and I had all weekend to woo my mate. My wolf was dying to go for a run, and despite my fatigue I figured it would be a good idea to wear him out a bit, so he'd quit bugging me about finding Cami.

I'd been messaging with her sister Pepper, getting intel on Cami's schedule so I could turn up when she least expected me. It was dishonest and maybe a bit stalkerish, but desperate times called for desperate measures. My phone rang with a text just as I was stripping down on my back porch. My house backed up against the forest, giving me great access to the wild areas that ringed Greysden. Since most of the people in town was shifters, it wasn't unusual to see someone wandering around in their animal form. Or coming home from a shift stark naked. I pulled out my phone.

Pepper: *We're having dinner on the patio at Ellery's if you want to drop by.*

Me: *Got it. Thanks.*

I was tempted to get dressed again and drive over to Ellery's, but decided a more subtle approach was warranted. In my wolf form, I could keep an eye on her without her knowing about it. I jumped off the porch, shifting mid-air. I felt the familiar pain of bones and muscles lengthening and changing shape as my canines pushed through my gums and my tail extended from the bottom of my spine. By the time my paws touched the grass, I was wearing my fur and eager to run. I let my wolf take control; he knew was to do.

Ellery's was about ten or twelve miles away from my house, and my wolf made quick work of running through the woods towards the restaurant. In this form, I could easily reach speeds of twenty-five to thirty miles an hour. I came out of the woods near Ellery's about fifteen minutes later. Sniffing the air, I quickly located my mate. The restaurant had a huge outdoor patio that was separated from the woods by an expanse of wild grass. I kept low, trying to avoid attracting too much attention. Keeping my eyes on my mate, I stalked closer.

I could tell the exact minute she realized I was there. Cami stiffened, then turned to scan the grass. Her eyes went right to where I was sneaking through the high grass. I'd felt the mate bond forming, the mystical connection between a shifter and their true mate, but I hadn't realized that she was feeling it too. She looked annoyed as she shot me a glare, then turned and said something to her sisters, both of whom shrugged with forced casualness.

I'd meant to watch her from afar, but my wolf wasn't having it. He wanted to get closer. He needed to get closer. Since Cami had already spotted me, I figured there was no use in hiding in the grass. Someone at a neighboring table gasped as I jumped lightly onto the patio, heading towards my mate.

"It's OK," Pepper called to her. "That's just our dog. He must have gotten out of the car."

"That's not a dog, it's a wolf," the lady protested. Sniffing the air, I realized she was human. Humans knew about shifters, but most of them were in denial. As shifters, we didn't flaunt our dual natures, and in return, most of the humans pretended that we didn't exist. It worked out fine for all of us.

"Yeah, we get that a lot," Pepper said, turning to me. "But wolves can't do this. Sit Stephen."

I dropped to my haunches, sitting down, and trying to make myself look small and unthreatening.

"Lay down."

Pepper pointed to the ground near their table, and I settled onto my stomach, paws under my muzzle as I stared at my mate. She studiously avoided my gaze.

"Good boy," Pepper said in that voice women used on animals. Internally I rolled my eyes, but I appreciated the assist. I hadn't thought it through when I decided to run over here wearing my fur.

Just then the waiter came by, giving me a disapproving frown. "No dogs on the porch, ladies."

"We were just leaving," Meri assured him. "Pepper, pay the check while Cami and I take Stephen to the car." She stood up and patted her leg. "Come on boy, let's go home and get your kibble."

This time it was Cami who rolled her eyes. I followed her and Meri to the car, and when Meri opened the back seat, I didn't wait for an invitation; I hopped right into the car.

"What are you doing?" Cami protested. "Run along now, Wolfie. You can't come with us."

I didn't move. Pepper came up and slid into the passenger seat before Cami could get there, forcing my mate to get in the backseat with me. She sighed deeply as she settled herself into the seat next to me. As soon as Meri started the car, I shifted forward to rest my head on her lap. To my surprise, Cami reached up and rubbed that spot between my ears that felt so good. The next thing I knew, I was fast asleep.

My mate stirring beneath my head woke me up. Her look was almost tender as she looked down at me.

"You're worn out, aren't you?"

It was obvious that she could sense my deep exhaustion through the mate bond. I nodded my wolf head, telling myself it was a good sign that she cared.

"All right then, you might as well come in for a while. I'm too tired to drive you back to Greysden, and I'm thinking you're too tired to run back yet." She pointed at me and gave me a stern look. "No funny business."

My wolf started panting excitedly as we jumped out of the car to follow our mate. The sun was setting, and there was a bit of a chill in the air as we walked into the house. Meri and Pepper were standing in the entryway, obviously spying on us. They looked gleeful.

"Why don't you take your boyfriend upstairs?" Pepper suggested with a mischievous look in her eyes.

I didn't wait for Cami to argue, I just padded upstairs. I heard her whispering with her sisters as I sniffed the floor and followed her scent to her bedroom. My mate came up behind me as I crossed over to the bed.

"What are you doing, Wolfie?"

Ignoring her, I hopped up on the bed, turned in a circle a couple of times, then laid down. Her bed was soft and comfortable, and it smelled like her. My wolf was in heaven. My eyes grew heavy again.

She sighed deeply. "OK, here's the deal. You can stay here tonight, but you need to stay in your wolf form so we're not tempted to do anything more than sleep. No sexy times for you, mister. I mean it."

I wagged my tail and snuggled into the comforter. I couldn't help but wonder who she was trying to keep away from temptation: me or her.

Cami went into the en-suite bathroom and returned a few minutes later wearing a pair of sweatpants and a giant sweatshirt that fell almost to her knees. I immediately felt a rush of jealousy as I wondered if she'd gotten the sweatshirt from one of her boyfriends. I was tempted to shift back to human to ask her about it, but honestly, I was just too exhausted. It was like I'd been on high alert the entire time we'd been separated, and now that we were together again, the adrenaline rush faded, and I was so sleepy I couldn't keep my eyes open.

Cami settled on the bed next to me, slipping underneath the covers and leaning against the headboard. She grabbed a remote control from the bedside table and switched on the television that was mounted to the wall.

"I'm going to share a deep, dark secret with you," she said. "I like to watch Scottish time travel romances." She started an on-demand video of a popular TV show, then reached over to rub my back. Before the opening credits finished, I was fast asleep again.

Cami

I woke up sweating. Was I getting night sweats already? I thought I had a couple of more years before menopause hit. I realized with a start that something was pressed against my back. Something big and warm and furry. It all came back to me. Dinner on the patio. Stephen popping up in the grass, then pretending to be a dog. Snuggling against his warm body as I watched my recorded shows until I fell asleep. Waking up next to Stephen in his wolf form was almost as fabulous as waking up next to him as a human. Minus the morning wood, of course.

After heading into the bathroom to pee and brush my teeth, I returned to find that Stephen had switched back into his human form and was reclining on the bed buck naked. Speaking of morning wood...

"What are you doing?" I asked. My voice was scratchy from sleep.

"Nothing," Stephen replied as he lazily scratched his chest. My eyes followed the movement. Damn these shifters aged well. I knew Stephen was forty, but he had the body of a twenty year old. A very hot, very fit twenty year old. Yum. My panties were immediately soaked, and I could tell by the smirk on his face and the flare of his nostrils that Stephen was well aware of that fact.

He crooked a finger at me, and without thinking I followed his unspoken command. As soon as I got close enough, he reached out his hand and pulled me towards the bed, rolling me onto my back underneath him before I even realized what had happened.

"What are you doing?" I asked again.

Stephen's smile was pure sin. "This."

His head descended slowly, giving me enough time to push him away. I knew I should, but I just couldn't do it. Not when I wanted to kiss him more than I wanted my next breath. After our night together I'd freaked out and pushed him away. What had happened with Frank made me doubt that I was a good judge of men anymore. But now, now I was tired of denying myself what I really wanted. Stephen. I knew logically that it was the magic spell bringing us together, but it felt so real to me.

His lips met mine, soft but firm, and I felt everything in my body relax. *This one.* I heard the words rumble through my body and in that moment, I let go of all of my reservations and kissed him back passionately. At least until I heard the pounding on the door.

"Chamomile? Honey, are you in there?"

I stiffened beneath Stephen. "Oh crap!"

Stephen was immediately on high alert. "Who is that? What's happening?"

I groaned. So much for my morning delight. "It's my mother. She's come home to reverse the love spell for us."

Stephen reared back, a flash of hurt passing through his eyes. "What?"

I rolled out from underneath him as my mother continued to pound on the door. "Hang on Mom," I called. "I'll be right out."

I turned back to explain to Stephen, "When I first realized that the spell had gone wrong, I emailed my mother to ask her to come home and fix it. I didn't want us to be bound because of a spell that was meant to help someone else. She and my father were traveling, Goddess knows where, so when I didn't hear back from her right away, I forgot all about it. I'm sure that's why she's here."

He pushed to his feet, his expression a mixture of disbelief and betrayal. "You asked another witch to undo our bond?"

I shook my head vigorously. "No, well, yes, kind of. I wanted to know if what we were feeling was because of the spell or if it was fate, like you say it is. I wanted to know if it was real."

"Is it really that bad being my mate that you have to use magic to make it go away? God, Cami. Were you even going to tell me about this?"

I'd never seen Stephen look so upset. I reached for him, but he backed away, heading for the door. "I can't believe you would do this to me, I can't believe you would do this to us."

He opened the door, nodding at my mother who shot him a wide-eyed look as she took in his naked body. A second later I heard his bare feet pounding down the stairs, quickly followed by the sound of the front door slamming as he ran out of the house. And out of my life, no doubt. My mother was here to fix this mess now. Once the spell was reversed, I had no doubt in my mind that the overwhelming connection we felt would be gone. And when the connection was gone, that would be it for us.

I pressed my hand against my mouth as my eyes filled with tears for the first time in years. Everything between us had just been the magic, I reminded myself. He'd never been mine to keep. Flinging myself into my mother's arms, I started to sob. My mother smoothed my hair, whispering words of comfort until I'd cried myself out, then grabbed my hand and pulled me to sit on the bottom of the bed.

"That was the guy? The wolf shifter who came after the spell and thinks you're his mate?"

I nodded.

"Why the tears, Chamomile? I thought you wanted out of this spell?"

"I did, but now I'm not so sure. I...I think I love him, but I'm not sure if it's genuine or I'm just wrapped up in the spell."

My mother shook her head. "What does it matter? If it's the spell, or if it's the call of the shifter's fated mate, it's all magic Chamomile. Love is its own magic."

"But the magic was meant for Pepper."

"The magic was meant for whomever it would serve most at this time. Clearly that was you."

"I can't live the rest of my life wondering if the man I love is with me because of free will, or because of some magic spell."

"You really love that wolf, don't you?" she asked.

I sniffed and felt the truth rush through me. "Yes."

"And yet you want to take a chance on the reversal spell making all that go away?"

"I guess, I mean, I think I do."

She raised one eyebrow, the same way she'd done when I was a child and said something ridiculous.

"I just need to know for sure Mom. I don't want to spend the rest of my life doubting his feelings for me." I didn't add that I had no doubt about my own feelings. They were real, and they would last even if he forgot all about me. I knew that as sure as I knew my own name.

Mom sighed deeply. "From what I've heard, there's nothing to doubt. But if you really want me to do a reversal, I can." She rubbed my shoulder. "But don't blame me if the magic doesn't work the way you hope it will."

Stephen

I ran through the woods as fast as my paws could carry me. My muscles bunched and lengthened as I flew past the trees headed for Greysden. For home.

Home is where Cami is, my wolf rebuked me.

"She doesn't want to be with us," I reminded us both. "That's why she wants her mother to undo her stupid love spell."

The betrayal hurt so much I could scarcely breathe. We had connected. I hadn't imagined that. And last night, something had shifted between us. As I lay curled up next to her in my wolf form, I could feel her resistance fading. I could feel the love in her touch as she absently stroked my fur while she watched her ridiculous TV shows. And when I'd awoken in the middle of the night, she had been curled around me, her head resting on my side as she slept peacefully.

What would happen after Mrs. Rosewater did the reversal spell, I wondered. Would I feel the same? Would she? Would we go back to being strangers living in neighboring towns, never knowing the other existed?

It's not a spell, she is our mate.

I hoped my wolf was right. Even if I forgot that Cami existed, I would still miss her on a cellular level. The connection with her was burned into my very soul. Even though I hadn't bitten her and claimed her, even though our mate bond hadn't been sealed yet, it was still there. It wouldn't be severed. Not completely.

If by some chance the spell actually broke the bond, I knew instinctively that I'd never be able to even look at another woman. The fates only brought one true mate for every shifter. Even if we didn't remember each other, I'd still mourn her loss. I would be doomed to spend the rest of my life all alone.

Not all alone, my wolf reminded me. My wolf sent me a series of images, like pictures in my mind. Me and Cami snuggled together in bed. A wedding ceremony in the clearing where we first met. The two of us sitting on the couch reading, both of us old and grey. I didn't know whether the images were wishful thinking or some kind of a vision of the future, but they gave me comfort.

"I hope you're right buddy."

By the time I got home, I was panting from the exertion of running full out for so long. I burst out of the woods into my back yard, making a beeline for my porch. I was running so fast I almost didn't notice the figure sitting on my back steps. Cami. I skidded to a stop, wondering if I was hallucinating.

Cami raised her hand in a half-hearted wave. I stalked towards her, watching her carefully. Her eyes were red and swollen. Clearly she had been crying. I exhaled sharply and called forth my human form. My fur receded, quickly followed by my claws and fangs, and my body reformed into my smaller human shape. I landed on my hands and knees in the grass, a few feet from my mate, breathing hard.

"What are you doing here?" I gasped.

"Can we talk for a few minutes?" she asked. "Please."

I walked past her on the porch and opened the back door, gesturing for her to follow me in. "I'll be right back."

I was dripping with sweat after my hard run, so I headed into the bathroom for a quick shower. The truth was, I needed some space too. If she was here to break it off, I needed to be prepared. After my shower, I brushed my teeth and pulled on some clothes, returning to find Cami in the living room. She was sitting on the couch, nervously twisting her hands in her lap. I plopped down on the other side of the couch, keeping distance between us, and remained silent, waiting for her to talk.

I couldn't decide how I was feeling. I'd been so hurt and betrayed by her plan to reverse the spell, even though I didn't believe that magic was involved in our connection. Not witch's magic anyway. Shifter magic was fated, and totally different. At least I hoped so. Honestly, it was her lack of faith that hurt me the most. But I also felt a sharp stab of fear.

If I was wrong and Cami was right, I was about to lose my fated mate. Just the thought of it made me want to burrow into a hole and lick my metaphorical wounds.

"I told my mother I didn't want her to reverse the spell."

My head popped up to stare at my mate in shock. "Why not?"

She scooted closer and I inhaled her sweet scent.

"I don't want to risk losing you," she whispered. "Even if we forgot all about each other, I still would miss you. The thing is…I love you, Stephen. I don't know if it's the spell or your shifter magic or just plain old human emotion. And I don't care. The only thing I care about is you, and us, and our future together." Her eyes filled with tears as she added, "That is, if you're still interested in a future with me."

My heart filled with joy, but I knew what I had to do…

"We're going through with the reversal spell," I said firmly, surprising both of us.

"What?"

"When I claim you as my mate – and make no mistake I will be claiming you, and soon – I don't want that damn spell hanging over our heads for the rest of our lives. I don't want you or anyone else to ever doubt that what we have is real, that we were brought together by fate, not by some stupid spell."

"But what if the spell breaks the connection between us?"

"That's a risk I'm willing to take Cami. I'm willing to risk it all because I know, in the end, we will be together, and you will be mine. And when your mother is done with the spell, you'll know it too. Then there will be no doubts remaining between us."

An hour later I was back at Cami's house. Mrs. Rosewater led the way to the clearing in the woods where I first ran into the sisters. Pepper and Meri walked side by side behind her, with me and Cami bringing up the rear. We walked hand-in-hand, and I could feel her start to tremble the closer we got.

Once we got there, I stood to the side while Cami's mom drew a circle in the dirt and placed various herbs and crystals in front of her. Pepper stacked some twigs, and her mom started a small fire with a flick of her wrist.

"I'm ready. You can all come to the circle now."

We gathered around the fire, sitting within the lines drawn in the dirt. Cami took one of my hands while Pepper took the other. Meri gasped loudly as Pepper grabbed her with her other hand.

"What is it?" Pepper asked. "What do you see?"

Meri rubbed her forehead, her eyes going glassy as a vision flashed in her mind. "A monster!"

We all stared at her as she mumbled incoherently for a few seconds. Her gaze cleared and she stared at her sister in shock. "Pepper! Your true love is a monster!"

"What are you talking about?" Pepper grabbed her hand again and squeezed. "Are you saying I'm going to fall in love with a terrible person? What the hell? Why do I have such bad luck in this damn clearing?"

"I don't know." Meri shook her head, as if clearing it. "I saw you in my vision, we were all in the library, and you were telling us you were in love, but he was a monster. It's all kind of hazy."

Pepper looked disturbed. "Oh for Goddess's sake, can we just get on with this spell reversal so I can go home and have a drink?"

Mrs. Rosewater looked between her daughters thoughtfully but didn't pry anymore. We all fell silent as she began to chant the magical incantations while she scattered ingredients into the fire. After a few moments, she pulled out a small vial with a green liquid in it and slid it towards Pepper.

"Drink this. It should flush the other potion out of your body."

The sisters looked at their mother in confusion. "Potion?" Pepper asked. "What potion?"

"The potion your sister gave you when she did the spell," Mrs. Rosewater explained.

"I didn't give her anything to drink," Cami said.

Pepper nodded. "Yeah, she just did the smoky herbs thing you're doing, right Meri?"

Meri nodded in confirmation. Mrs. Rosewater sat back on her heels and started to laugh. We all looked at each other, even more confused.

"What's so funny?" Cami asked her mother.

"You didn't complete the spell."

"I don't understand."

"You only did the first part of the spell Chamomile. It's like you knocked at the door but didn't go inside."

I raised my hand like I was in school. "Can you explain that more clearly for the non-magical folks here please?"

Mrs. Rosewater pinned me with an intense look. "The first part of the spell creates an environment where the participants are receptive. It's a heart opening spell. But for it to also bring love, the person who wants to be matched needs to also drink the love potion. No love potion, no love spell."

She turned her gaze to her oldest daughter. "The magic softened your heart Chamomile, but Stephen came to you because of fate, not because of the spell."

I pumped my fist in the air like I'd just scored the winning touchdown in the Super Bowl. "Told you!" I crowed to Cami. "Shifter magic for the win!"

I leapt to my feet, dragging her up with me, then tossed her over my shoulder like I'd done that day I'd spirited her away from her store.

"What are you doing?" she laughed as I took off running. I tightened my arm around her thighs to keep her from falling off.

"We're going home Cami. I'm not going to waste another day without my mate mark on your neck."

"But..."

I smacked her ass smartly. "No more excuses Chamomile Ginseng Rosewater. Tonight, you will be mine."

And she was.

Epilogue—Cami

Four months later...

"Happy anniversary!"

I looked around at all the people gathering in the backyard at Rosewater manor. It seemed like the whole town had come out to celebrate my parents' fortieth anniversary. My sister Meri had outdone herself planning this party; she had always loved organizing social events. The yard had been completely transformed into a party venue with long tables laden with food, a seating area, games for the kids, even a dance floor.

"Thank you," Mom said, leaning into to wrap me and Stephen into a warm hug. "I'm glad you could make it."

"Like we would miss this," Stephen said. "My parents should be here soon too."

There had been a lot of changes in my life over the past few months. I'd moved in with Stephen right after we mated, and a few weeks later we got married, opting to have a small intimate ceremony in the clearing where we'd first met. Sometimes I missed living at Rosewater Manor, but I couldn't deny that I loved living with my mate.

Our lives had meshed together surprisingly well. His family had welcomed me into the fold wholeheartedly, and his parents had become good friends with my own parents. We'd even adopted a cat that had turned up in our yard one day. She was still a little nervous about Stephen, but she'd definitely warmed up to him. Life was good.

Stephen and I made our way over to where Cami and Meri were standing, watching the guests mingle.

"Hey girls, what's new?"

My sisters both greeted me with a hug. "I'm going to Denver for a Samhain retreat," Pepper told us, referring to the Wiccan holiday that coincided with Halloween. "I want to get in touch with my inner Goddess."

Meri rolled her eyes behind Pepper's back but didn't say anything.

"That sounds fun," I said encouragingly. "I…"

I stopped as I saw Meri grab her head. "What is it, Meri? What do you see?"

"Whiteness falls from the sky," she gasped. Having a vision always made her head hurt.

"It's a little early for snow, Turmeric," Pepper teased.

Just then we heard a screech. We whirled around just in time to see two kids crash into the table where the cake was. Meri had insisted on getting my parents a ridiculously expensive wedding cake for their anniversary. They hit the table just at the right angle to make it tip forward. The cake flew up in the air before falling to the ground in a shower of white frosting.

"Whiteness falls from the sky all right," Stephen laughed.

I poked him in the side, and he pivoted to pull me into his arms. He pressed a kiss to the scar on my neck, the spot where he marked me as his mate. The spot throbbed beneath his lips. I pushed him a way with a laugh, but he looped his arms around me, holding me close.

"I love you, Chamomile."

I looked up into his eyes and saw the truth shining there. The bond between us was real, and it was its own kind of magic. "I love you too, Wolfie."

***

Thank you for reading "Love Potion". If you liked this book, please leave a review.

Coming soon: Pepper and Meri find their own love matches. Be sure to sign up for my mailing list[1] to be notified when the rest of the Magical Midlife series releases. I'll even give you a free book! In the meantime, read about how Stephen's boss Stuart finds his own mate in "Kat's Dog", available everywhere here.[2]

1.　　https://storyoriginapp.com/giveaways/62ee758e-068f-11eb-904e-c373f6014fe1

2.   https://books2read.com/u/bxeXQq

Special Preview

Until You Came Along by Rose Bak

Jen heard the rumbling from all the way in the kitchen. Wiping her hands on a towel, she walked to the front porch to watch the two large buses drive up the long driveway to the farmhouse. Belching smoke, they idled and came to a stop, one behind the other.

Although it wasn't even 10 a.m. yet, the sun shone brightly in the summer sky, showcasing the dust left in the wake of the parked buses. A bird squawked loudly in the sudden silence as a serious looking young woman scurried out of the first bus, glasses askew, a clipboard gripped in one hand, cellphone in another. Two large mountains of men followed her, hulking shadows.

"Jen Oliver? The band is here. We'll just come in and...." she moved to enter the house, but Jen stood her ground, blocking the door.

"Where are they?" she asked the woman, her tone icy. "And who are you exactly?"

The woman looked flustered for a brief moment before her stern mask fell back down again. She shuffled her cell phone into the hand with the clipboard and stuck out her now-free hand to shake. "I'm Simone. I manage the band."

Jen ignored her hand. "Well, manage them out of those buses. They don't get to send the help out to greet their sister."

Simone looked confused as she dropped her hand back to her side. "They're all sleeping. They had a late night. We'll just come in and check...."

"Still up all night and sleeping all day, huh? That's been the same since they were teenagers." Jen shook her head. On the farm they had all been taught the value of hard work – up before dawn, work all day, and early to bed. Somehow those lessons hadn't really stuck with her brothers despite her grandparents' best efforts over the years.

Of course, the boys, as she still thought of them, had been away from the farm for ten years now, chasing fame and fortune as the biggest boy band to hit the charts since N Sync. Like the band that came before them, the Oliver Boys had grown up but continued to enchant teenage girls across the world with their pop tunes.

Simone clearly felt protective of the boys. "They played last night in Wichita you know," she said sternly. "The show went until almost midnight, then they met the fans and press for hours after."

"By meet the fans and press do you mean got drunk and partied?" Jen's tone did little to hide her opinion of the boys and their reputation for debauched partying.

Simone shook her head. "They've mostly settled down now. There's not as much partying as there used to be when they were younger. But they still need to make an effort to meet people, it's part of the job. Now we'll just come in and...."

Jen shook her head. "Well," she drawled. "When they wake up from their so-called job, you send them on in. The rest of you need to find some other place to bunk. I'm not running a hotel for drunken roadies here."

A slight movement behind Simone caught Jen's eyes. One of the giant men flanking Simone shook with repressed laughter, his mouth twisted in a smirk but his face otherwise impassive. Jen looked at him for the first time. He was the size of a small tank, several inches over six feet tall, with impossibly wide shoulders and large biceps. His hair was a dark blond, "dishwater blonde" her grandma would call it, worn military short. He was dressed all in black, and she noticed a gun on the shoulder holster. Jen wondered why he felt he needed a gun out here in the middle of nowhere. She felt him watching her and she raised her eyes to his, a shiver of awareness coursing through her, although she couldn't make out his eyes behind the dark sunglasses.

"Miss Oliver..." Simone started again.

"Jen"

"OK, then, Jen, we need to do a security sweep before the boys come in. If you could just move aside, we'll get started." Simone nodded decisively.

"A security—-what the hell are you talking about?"

Simone turned to the man who'd been staring at Jen earlier. "This is Nick, he's head of security for the band. He'll be doing a security sweep and assessment with Brian here," she pointed at the second silent man.

"We don't need a security sweep. This place is as safe as it comes. We don't even lock the doors in these parts."

Simone shook her head again, vibrating with irritation and clearly not used to people disobeying her orders. "No way. The boys don't go anywhere without a security check ahead of time. I'm afraid I have to insist."

Jen shot her a look filled with venom, her tone as cold as ice. "You can insist all you like but this is my property. You have no right to it, and neither do the boys. Y'all can just run along now, I'm not having some ginormous strangers poking around my property. Don't make me sic the dogs on you." Simone's mouth dropped open.

This was an empty threat. Jen's three dogs looked mean, but they were incurably friendly. They were just as likely to lick a person to death as bite them. Jen had a sneaking suspicion that if someone tried to kill her the dogs would jump over her body and leave with the killer. But these music people didn't need to know that. If there was one thing Jen hated, it was music people. They were way too self-important and proud.

"Excuse me ma'am," the guy called Nick interrupted.

"Jen," she repeated, a trace of irritation in her tone.

He inclined his head. "Sorry. Jen. As Simone mentioned, I'm head of security for the band. We've had some issues and I would be very appreciative if my team could just poke around for a bit and make sure there's nothing amiss." His tone was deferential and charming, which only heightened Jen's suspicions.

"What kind of issues?"

"I'm afraid I'm not at liberty to discuss that ma—I mean Jen."

"Then I'm afraid I'm not at liberty to grant you access to my property. You step foot off that driveway, and I'll shoot you myself, right after I set the dogs on you. And you," she pointed at Simone, "better make sure no one bothers me again until I see those boys on my porch." She spun on her heel and slammed the door. It was going to be a long day.

***

*For more of Jen's story, check out **Until You Came Along** by Rose Bak. Available at select online retailers.*

Other Books by Rose Bak

Boozy Book Club Series
Beach Reads
Bubbly & Billionaires
Martinis & Mysteries
Bourbon & Bikers
Midlife Madness
Magical Midlife Series
Love Potion
Psychic Flashes
The Good with Numbers Holiday Romance Series
Love Unmasked
The Thanksgiving Scrooge
Maid for Christmas
Countdown to Love
Valentine's Lottery
Christmas Angel
Bite-Sized Shifters Paranormal Romance Series
Long Distance Wolf
Wolf Doctor
Kat's Dog
Designer Wolf
Wolf Sheriff
Cocktail Wolf
Second Chance Wolf
The Oliver Boys Band Contemporary Romance Series
Until You Came Along
Rock Star Teacher
Rock Star Writer
Rock Star Neighbor
Rock Star Lawyer

Loving the Holidays Contemporary Romance Series
Dating Santa
New Year's Steve
Independence Dave
Comfort & Joy
Holidays with the Shifters Series
Santa's Claws
Bear Humbug
Jingle Bear
Silver Paws
Joy to the Wolf
Lion's Heart
The Diamond Bay Contemporary Romance Series
Brand New Penny
Fresh as a Daisy
Right as Rain
Reunited Series
Together Again
Finding My Baby
Standalones
Beach Wedding
Jessie's Girl
Summer Wedding
Faking It with the Detective
Roasting with Rob
King of the Reunion
Saving Texas
Non-fiction
What to Do If You Find a Cougar in Your Living Room: Self-Care in an Uncaring World
It's All About Relationships: Reflections on Love, Friendship, and Connection

Catch up with these and other stories coming soon. Join my newsletter for more information[1] or follow my author page on your favorite retailer.

---

1. https://storyoriginapp.com/giveaways/62ee758e-068f-11eb-904e-c373f6014fe1

About the Author

Rose Bak has been obsessed with books since she got her first library card at age five. She is a passionate reader with an e-reader bursting with thousands of beloved books.

Although Rose enjoys writing both fiction and nonfiction, romance novels have always been her favorite guilty pleasure, both as a reader and an author. Rose's contemporary romance books focus on strong female characters over thirty-five and the alpha males who love them. Expect a lot of steam, a little bit of snark, and a guaranteed happily ever after.

Rose lives in the Pacific Northwest with her family, and special needs dogs. In addition to writing, she also teaches accessible yoga and loves music. Sadly, she has absolutely no musical talent, so she mostly sings in the shower.

Please sign up for the Rose Bak Romance newsletter[1] to get a free book and keep up to date on all the latest news.

You can also follow Rose on Facebook[2], Instagram[3], Twitter[4], Goodreads[5], or Bookbub[6].

---

1. https://storyoriginapp.com/giveaways/62ee758e-068f-11eb-904e-c373f6014fe1

2. https://www.facebook.com/AuthorRoseBak

3. https://www.instagram.com/authorrosebak/

4. https://twitter.com/AuthorRoseBak

5. https://www.goodreads.com/authorrosebak

6. https://www.bookbub.com/authors/rose-bak

Don't miss out!

Visit the website below and you can sign up to receive emails whenever Rose Bak publishes a new book. There's no charge and no obligation.

https://books2read.com/r/B-A-VATM-EHCAC

BOOKS 2 READ

Connecting independent readers to independent writers.

Did you love *Love Potion*? Then you should read *Wolf Doctor*[7] by Rose Bak!

[8]

Wolf Doctor: A Paranormal Romantic Comedy

When wolf shifter Colt Hanson plunges off a cliff, he's expecting to be roadkill. Fortunately, someone mistakes him for a dog and brings him to the town's veterinary clinic. He's not happy about waking up in a dog kennel, but when he opens his eyes and sees his fated mate, he knows things are finally looking up.Dr. Valerie Lupa doesn't believe in fated mates or any kind of mates for that matter. She's an independent wolf and she likes her life just the way it is. There's no way she's going to submit to Colt, no matter what her wolf side is telling her.As the two shifters sniff around each other, the pull of their attraction proves too much to resist. With a little help from their friends, they just might be

---

7. https://books2read.com/u/4AOXXK

8. https://books2read.com/u/4AOXXK

able to dip their paws into a relationship that will last longer than the full moon."Wolf Doctor" is book one in the "Bite-Sized Shifters", a series of paranormal romantic comedies you can read in just a few hours. Each book in the series is standalone featuring a mature couple, steamy scenes, a lot of fur and claws, and a guaranteed HEA.

Read more at https://rosebakenterprises.com/.

www.ingramcontent.com/pod-product-compliance
Lightning Source LLC
Chambersburg PA
CBHW031457130726

47989CB00003B/1434